The Big Apple Effect

Christy Goerzen

Orca currents

ORCA BOOK PUBLISHERS

Library and Archives Canada Cataloguing in Publication

Goerzen, Christy, 1975-, author
The Big Apple effect / Christy Goerzen.
(Orca currents)

Issued in print and electronic formats.
ISBN 978-1-4598-0739-6 (bound).--ISBN 978-1-4598-0738-9 (pbk.).--
ISBN 978-1-4598-0740-2 (pdf).--ISBN 978-1-4598-0741-9 (epub)

I. Title. II. Series: Orca currents
PS8613.O38B53 2014   jc813'.6   c2014-901561-5
                           c2014-901562-3

First published in the United States, 2014
Library of Congress Control Number: 2014935379

Summary: Fifteen-year-old Maddie has won an art contest
and gets to visit New York City.

*Orca Book Publishers is dedicated to preserving the environment and has
printed this book on Forest Stewardship Council® certified paper.*

Orca Book Publishers gratefully acknowledges the support for its
publishing programs provided by the following agencies: the Government
of Canada through the Canada Book Fund and the Canada Council for the Arts,
and the Province of British Columbia through the BC Arts Council
and the Book Publishing Tax Credit.

Cover photography by Shutterstock

ORCA BOOK PUBLISHERS
PO Box 5626, Stn. B
Victoria, BC Canada
V8R 6S4

ORCA BOOK PUBLISHERS
PO Box 468
Custer, WA USA
98240-0468

www.orcabook.com
Printed and bound in Canada.

17 16 15 14 • 4 3 2 1

To Chay,
one of the brightest lights in my life

Chapter One

"You will meet a handsome stranger soon," my mother's voice floated out from behind layers of red velvet. "Love is coming to you. Just open your heart." I brushed aside the velvet scarves that hung from the living room ceiling. Crystals on long strings clinked together.

I stuck my head in and immediately coughed from all the incense smoke.

"Mom—I mean, Lady Venus—are you almost done?" I said. "I have to be at the airport in an hour."

"Maddie," my mom said, gold bangles clattering on her wrists, "don't interrupt me while I'm with a client." She smiled apologetically at the woman across the table covered with tarot cards and candles. I recognized my mom's client as a cashier from our local Safeway.

I sighed and paced around the kitchen. My suitcase was packed with my best outfits. My passport, plane ticket and American money were tucked into my red patent leather purse. I was ready to go. All I needed was for my mom to drive me to the airport.

I couldn't sit down. I was way too excited. I was going to the city of my dreams, New York, for one whole week. I had wanted to go to there since I was ten years old, after I read the book *Harriet the Spy*.

But the best part was that I was traveling without my mom, for the first time ever. My whole life my mom had made me go on summer "adventures," as she called them. These adventures usually involved raw food, or reiki, or drum circles, or some awful combination of the three. In other words, not exactly what the average teenager finds thrilling.

Last summer's adventure had turned out to be the best one yet, even though I had been sure it would be one of the worst. My mom had arranged for us to volunteer for a week on an organic farm with cows, goats and prizewinning garlic. It didn't take long for my mom to totally embarrass me. Her New Age ways didn't exactly fit in with the ways of old-school farmers.

Luckily, though, those farmers had a daughter the same age as me: Anna. It was because of her that I got first runner-up in a contest run by my favorite art magazine, *Canvas*. My prize also included $500 and an all-access pass to all of New York City's art galleries. While in New York my art was going to be part of a big art gallery show, with art critics, agents and world-famous artists there. My hero, artist Louise Bergville, was a special invited guest.

This was going to be the best week of my life, I just knew it.

After I paced around the kitchen for ten more minutes, my mother finally emerged from behind the scarves.

"Thank you for coming to see me," she said in her Lady Venus voice, which was like her regular voice except that she drew out her vowels. "All the best in your search for true love." When she was in Lady Venus mode, she also widened her black-lined eyes. It looked ridiculous.

The door clicked shut behind her client.

"She'll never find a man until she waxes her upper lip," my mom chortled, ruffling the sheaf of twenty-dollar bills the woman had handed over. As much as my mother liked to think she was enlightened, she could be shallow.

Then Mom looked up. Her eyes filled with tears, as they had so many times the past weeks. "Oh, honey, I can't believe the day has finally come. You're flying off with your own two wings."

"I'm actually flying off with Air Canada's two wings," I said, my voice louder than it needed to be. "If I make it!"

"Do I have time to change?" my mom asked.

"No, you do not!" I said. I was already holding my bags. "You're driving me to the airport as Lady Venus. I have to be there in forty-five minutes." I was willing to risk embarrassment in order to get to the airport in time.

"Okay, okay," Mom said. She picked up her purse and started rooting for her keys. "Where are they? I know they're in here…" she muttered.

"Mom, are you stalling on purpose?" I said. I shifted from one foot to another and looked at the clock. Missing my flight was not an option.

"Here they are," my mother sang triumphantly two minutes later, jingling her keys in the air. Considering that she had a gigantic quartz crystal on the key chain, it was amazing that she lost them so often.

We headed out to the alley and climbed into my mom's old car, which she called Dave. Dave was a backfiring, stalling, blue-smoke-blowing hunk of metal, but Mom loved him.

Along the way, Mom went on and on about how much she was going to miss me. "It doesn't seem right that I'm not there for your birthday."

"Don't worry," I said. "We'll celebrate when I get back." Whatever it took for her to stop talking and hurry up.

After overheating on a bridge and stalling at an intersection, we reached the International Departures terminal with only two minutes to spare. I used words for Dave that my mom had never heard me say before.

"We're here!" Mom said, pulling up on the sidewalk as Dave lurched and stalled. A family entering the terminal leapt out of the way in fright.

And there was Anna, near the doors. It had been a year since I'd seen her. With her chin raised slightly in the air, she looked as calm and cool as always. She had flown from Kelowna by herself. Now she and I would fly together to New York.

Anna walked up to my car window.

"Hey," she said. "You're late."

I was sweaty and out of breath from nerves. "I know, I'm sorry. My mom's stupid car—" I said, unbuckling my seat belt and clambering out.

"It's okay, nerd" Anna smiled and punched me in the shoulder. She peered into the car at my mom in her Lady Venus getup. "Hi, Mrs. Turner," she said.

Mom jumped out and hurried to wrap her arms around me. Her bracelets clanged loudly in my ears as she smothered me in a hug.

"Goodbye, my dear daughter. See you soon." She paused, giggling. "I mean, in a week." Then she hugged Anna, who gave a weak effort.

"Mom, we gotta go," I said.

"Let me make sure I have all of your brother's contact information," Mom said, taking out her phone. "You know, in case of emergency. So it's 1153 Bleecker Street, New York, phone number—"

My mom could draw things out forever. I looked at my watch. We had exactly one minute to get to the check-in desk.

"Mom, you've asked that a million times," I said, grabbing my bags. "See you in a week."

"It's just that I'm going to miss you so much, honey. Love you!" she called after me as we rushed into the terminal.

I ran a few steps and then looked back quickly. Mom was still waving at us from the car. She looked a little lonely, standing there all by herself.

"Love you," I called back, but the terminal doors had already shut.

Chapter Two

"I can't wait to see my Big Apple outfit!" Anna said. We had checked in, gone through security, and were at the departure gate.

"You may be wearing your usual jeans and T-shirt now," I said, rummaging around in my carry-on, "but in a moment you will look *fabulous*." Anna and I had spent hours on the phone the night before, with me describing various clothes to her. Together, we decided on a perfect New York City outfit.

I pulled out the carefully rolled bundle and laid the outfit out on the seat between us. It was a short skirt with a graffiti print, plus little black boots and a black tank top.

Anna touched the hem of the skirt. "This is even better than I imagined," she said. "It's kind of punk rock."

"*Now boarding disabled passengers at Gate Four*," a crackly voice said over the loudspeaker. "*Other passengers, we'll be boarding at Gate Four in five minutes.*"

"Do you think I have time?" Anna said.

"Go, hurry!" I said.

Anna grabbed the clothes and ran to the bathroom. Moments later, she dashed back out. She'd pulled her long red hair into a messy high ponytail. The skirt and tank top fit her perfectly.

"I love it," she said, spinning around.

"You look amazing," I said.

"So do you," Anna said, admiring my vintage yellow and white shift dress. I'd bought it especially for the trip.

"Anna, do you realize that in five hours we'll be in New York City?"

"I can't believe it's actually happening," she said.

We whooped and danced around in the waiting area. We didn't care if people stared.

Ten minutes later, we were in our seats on the airplane. I cracked open my notebook.

"Let's go over our lists again!" I said, holding up my opened notebook for Anna to see.

"Uh, lists?" Anna said, glancing at my notebook.

"You know how we've been talking for months about all the things we want to do in New York? Don't you have it written down?"

"No," Anna said simply.

"Oh," I said, disappointed. I'd spent hours putting my list together.

"My list is all up here," Anna said, tapping her temple.

"Okay, well, can I read you my list again?" I said with a small squeal. "I've added stuff to it since last time."

"You mean since you read it to me last night?" she asked.

"Yup," I said.

"Maddie," Anna said, "calm down. You look a little crazed around the eyes." She laughed.

"It's just that I've wanted to go to New York since I was ten," I said. "I'm like a little kid on Christmas morning. Can you believe the art opening is only five sleeps away?"

"I know! It's amazing," Anna said, grabbing my knee. "And I get to be your date. It'll be so fancy."

"In only four days I'll get to meet Louise Bergville," I said. "This could be my big break in the art scene," I continued.

"I can't wait." Anna folded her arms behind her head, settling in. She smiled over at me. "All right. Let's go over this list again."

"Did I tell you I also made a color-coded map?" I carefully unfolded the New York City map that I'd been working on for months. I had marked numbers on it that corresponded to the numbers on my list. "Blue for art galleries, red for restaurants, yellow for shopping…"

"Wow," Anna said, staring at the map. "That's really, uh, intricate."

Sometimes I felt like an overexcited dork next to Anna.

I took a deep breath. "Number one. Vintage clothes shopping at the following stores: Screaming Mimi's, Beacon's Closet, Vice Versa—"

"You don't have to read out *all* the names," Anna said. "But they do sound fun."

"We *have* to find me the perfect art-show outfit for the *Canvas* event," I said.

"Mega priority, I know," Anna said, placing a reassuring hand on my arm. "Maybe I can find something too," she added with a small giggle.

"Maybe," I said as I flipped the page.

"Number two," I went on. "Visit the following art galleries: the Museum of Modern Art, the Guggenheim, the Pace Gallery, Bronx Museum of the Arts…"

"Wow," Anna peered over my shoulder at the list. "That's a lot of galleries."

"And look, I wrote down all the addresses, with corresponding subway stops."

"I love it," Anna said. "Go on."

"Number three. Eat a pastrami sandwich in a delicatessen."

"I want to do that too," Anna said. "I bet Thomas knows all the good ones."

"Number four. See an off-Broadway play."

"*On*-Broadway," Anna said. "None of that weirdo off-Broadway stuff."

"Don't tell me you want to see *Phantom of the* freaking *Opera* or something," I said.

Anna squirmed. "I have kind of wanted to see that one."

I made a face. "There is no way I'll be dragged into any sort of Andrew Lloyd Webber production."

Anna recovered quickly. "Snob," she said, elbowing me in the ribs.

"Country bumpkin tourist," I said, elbowing her back.

We giggled.

"Number five," I continued to read from my list. "Drink coffee in a Greenwich Village café."

"Easy." Anna nodded. "We'll be there."

While in New York we were going to stay with Anna's nineteen-year-old brother, Thomas. He lived in Greenwich Village, which was so cool I could hardly believe it was true. He'd been there for a year, studying math at Columbia University.

I continued to read from my list.

"Number thirty-five—" I said.

"How long is this list now, anyway?" Anna asked.

"It goes up to one hundred and thirty-four," I said.

Anna's eyes widened. She took her phone out of her pocket and tapped the screen, calculating. "Do you realize that's an average of 19.14 things per day?"

"We can do it," I said.

"Did you add anything in there about shopping at Saks Fifth Avenue and seeing a Yankees game?" Anna said. "You know that's what I want to do."

"We might be able to do those things," I said. "If we have time. Now, as I was saying, number thirty-five—"

"Maddie," Anna yawned. "I think I've had enough for now." She turned away from me, closing her eyes.

"Oh," I said, fiddling with the corner of my notebook page. I read the list to myself again, for possibly the thousandth time.

I ate a little bag of peanuts and watched an episode of *Mr. Bean*. After that, I decided to take a nap too. I might as well rest up before we arrived.

For the past month or so I'd had a recurring dream where Anna and I had a picnic on the top of the Statue of Liberty's head. The picnic was complete with wicker basket, sandwiches and a red-and-white checked blanket. It was always warm and breezy, and we looked through the statue's spiked crown at an amazing view of the whole city.

I tipped my head back in my seat and closed my eyes, and I was there again. I let myself drift off.

A sharp jostling of my arm brought me out of my dream.

"Maddie, look!" Anna said.

Rubbing my eyes, I leaned over Anna. I gasped. There she was, in the flesh. Or should I say, in the metal. We were flying over the Statue of Liberty's head, with a view of the city stretching out in front of us. The twilit sky was deep navy with a full, bright moon. All of New York sparkled.

"*This is your co-pilot speaking,*" a scratchy voice said over the PA. "*We are now descending into LaGuardia Airport.*

It is 10:04 PM local time, and the weather is beautiful."

We had arrived. My big adventure was about to begin.

Chapter Three

"There he is," Anna said, pointing out a tall, dark-haired guy near the baggage claim. He waved at us.

"Thomas!" Anna cried.

He had shaggy hair, a red hoodie and skinny dark jeans. *Cute*. He swept Anna up and spun her around in a hug.

"Sis! It's so good to see you!" he said.

"Thanks for making the trek all the way to the big city for little old me."

"I didn't come to see you," Anna said, grinning. "I came for the shopping."

"Nice clothes." Thomas whistled, giving Anna the once-over. "A departure from your usual."

"Courtesy of Maddie," Anna said, gesturing toward me.

"Nice to meet you, Maddie," Thomas said, shaking my hand. His was large and warm.

"I saw your prizewinning picture," Thomas continued. "I don't know much about art, but your portrait is amazing."

I blushed. "Thanks," I said. Anna's brother was cute *and* nice.

Our bags spun past on the baggage claim belt—my vintage brown leather suitcase and Anna's black suitcase on wheels.

"Only one suitcase each?" Thomas said, whisking our suitcases off the belt. "I thought girls overpacked."

"I have an extra bag in my suitcase for all the clothes I'm going to buy while I'm here," I explained.

"I didn't have that many clothes to bring," Anna said matter-of-factly.

"This way," Thomas said, as he led us out of the airport.

My phone buzzed in my pocket again. As we'd gotten off the plane my phone had immediately buzzed with six texts from my mom. **R u there? Maddie? R u there now? I miss u! Love u! Text me back!** I hadn't written back yet.

Now it said: **I'm worried! U should have arrived by now.**

I hurriedly typed back: **Yes! All good!**

I ran to catch up with Anna and Thomas, who were headed for the subway to take us into Manhattan. As we stepped outside the airport, I paused and breathed deeply. *I am inhaling authentic New York City air*, I thought.

"Hey, I'm walkin' here!" I heard a gruff voice shout from behind me. A real New York accent!

"Hey, girlie!" someone else shouted. "Move it!"

I snapped back to reality and looked around. Who were they talking to?

"She's moving, all right?" Anna shouted, pulling me next to her.

I felt my face flush. Unfortunately, I had chosen to stop right in the way of people trying to board the escalator.

Anna clucked her tongue as two men dressed in business suits rushed past us.

"Anna, you sounded like you were in a movie just now," I said, trying to bounce back.

"Thanks," Anna said. "I figure while in New York, do as the New Yorkers do."

"Not bad," Thomas said, clearly impressed.

We rode the subway into Manhattan. The subway car was crowded, so Anna, Thomas and I stood in the middle, hanging on to straps that hung down from the ceiling.

"Here's the Delancey Street station," Thomas said brightly. "Our stop."

"Maddie wants to go to a delicatessen," Anna said, as we took the stairs to street level.

"Let's go to Katz's," Thomas said. "They have the best pastrami sandwiches there. Perfect for a late-night bite."

My heart fluttered. Katz's Delicatessen had been in loads of movies.

Dazzled, I followed Thomas. I couldn't help staring at everything and everyone. Taxi cabs whizzed by, many of them honking. These were real yellow New York City cabs, not boring, black Vancouver ones. Impossibly fashionable women clacked by in high heels. I didn't see a single pair of yoga pants. Brownstone buildings with funky shops and cafés lined every street. It was so much busier, so much more alive than back home.

Once inside Katz's, I found that I could check not only number three off my list—visit a delicatessen—but also number forty, which was to drink to a real egg cream. I'd read about egg creams in the *Lonely Planet Guide to New York City*. Basically, it was milk and chocolate syrup mixed with club soda to make it foamy. No eggs, despite the name. It was a must-have NYC classic.

We found a table in the crowded deli and set down our plates. I was the only one to order an egg cream. Thomas and Anna got boring old glasses of water.

I felt my phone buzz. I groaned.

"*Another* text from your mom?" Anna said, as I took out my phone. "I'm so glad my parents don't have cell phones."

How is it?! the text from my mom said.

I paused, staring at my screen. **Amazing**, I wrote. I vowed not to look at my phone any more that night, even if it buzzed.

I took my notebook and pen out of my bag. I opened to my list and put tick marks next to numbers three and forty.

"What's that?" Thomas nodded toward my notebook.

"Oh," I said. I suddenly felt shy about my list. "It's, um, my list of things I want to do while we're here."

"It goes up to one hundred and thirty-four," Anna said.

"Hmmm," Thomas said. "That's an average of 19.14 things per day."

"Whoa, you can figure that out in your hea—"

"See, this is what I was telling her," Anna interrupted me. I guessed she was used to her brother's math prowess.

"Might be a little ambitious," Thomas said, through a bite of his sandwich. "What's number seventy-seven?"

"Why number seventy-seven?" I said.

"We recently discussed Gaussian distribution in my Popular Proofs class," Thomas said with a shrug.

I looked at Anna blankly.

"Translation?" Anna said to Thomas.

"Just being random," Thomas said. He turned back to me. "So, number seventy-seven?"

"Attend a church service in Harlem," I said. "I heard the singing is amazing."

"Interesting," Thomas said. "Number one hundred and twelve?"

"See a band at Roseland," I said.

"You have to be twenty-one," Thomas said, frowning. "It's in a bar. Sorry."

"Oh," I said. I crossed it off the list. Then, I took a sip from my big glass of egg cream.

"How's the drink?" Anna said.

"Pretty good." I didn't want to admit that it was kind of gross. I forgot that I couldn't stand the taste of club soda. At least the pastrami sandwich was tasty.

"Well," Thomas said, "you've already checked two things off the list. Let's see if we can't get to the other 17.14 things we need to do today."

My heart melted a little every time Thomas spoke. *No, Maddie*, I thought. *It would be wrong to develop a crush on your friend's brother.* Wrong or not, it was happening.

"Come on, ladies," he said. He stuck his hands in his pockets and crooked his elbows out for us to each place a hand in, one on either side. "Let's rock this town."

Chapter Four

After the deli we made our way to Thomas's apartment to leave our bags. Luckily it was only a few streets away. My suitcase had lost its cool vintage appeal once I realized how annoying and heavy it was to carry. I'd already whacked two people with it by accident. I wanted Anna's sleek rolling one.

"Here we are," Thomas said, stopping at the front door of a tall, narrow brick building. For about the hundredth time that day, I felt an excited shudder run down my back. Thomas's apartment building was a classic New York walk-up, just like in the movies and TV shows.

"Ta-da!" he said, throwing open his front apartment door.

Anna and I peered in. There was a sink, a tiny fridge, two chairs and a math-related poster on the wall. A futon couch butted against a milk crate with a lamp on it. The whole apartment wasn't much bigger than my bedroom at home.

"Bathroom's that way," Thomas pointed down the hall.

"You don't have a bathroom in your apartment?" Anna said, her mouth gaping open. "Do Mom and Dad know?"

Thomas looked down. "Nope," he said quietly. My heart swelled. Gosh, he was cute when he was sheepish.

"Early mornings are the best time to take a shower," he added. "There's usually hot water then."

Okay, so we had to share a toilet. Big deal. This place was *awesome*. Very bohemian.

"I'll sleep on an air mattress on the floor," Thomas said. "And you two can share the futon. It folds out pretty big."

"Where are you going to fit, in the sink?" Anna said. "There's no room on the floor."

I didn't think Anna was acting very nicely toward Thomas.

"I think it's perfect," I piped up. "I love it." I touched Thomas's arm lightly.

Before I knew it, Anna stepped on my toe, hard. "Ow!" I said.

Thomas didn't seem to notice. "Sam's band the Smudges is playing at the Green Room Café tonight. Want to go?"

"Going to a Greenwich Village coffeehouse is number five on my list!" I exclaimed.

"I thought so," Thomas said. "Anna?"

"Sure," Anna shrugged. "I've been wanting to meet Sam, anyway."

This was exciting. I bet the band was a bunch of other cute New York boys. They had to be, if Thomas was friends with them.

"Dump your bags, and let's go," Thomas said.

An hour later, I was in bliss. I was sitting between Thomas and Anna in a cool coffeehouse. Right in front of us, the Smudges were playing. I couldn't help stealing looks at Thomas every few seconds. Thomas, meanwhile, was staring at the band.

The band sounded kind of folk pop. I was more of a punk fan, but they were pretty good. The guitarist and the drummer were both college-type guys with shaggy hair. The singer was a super-cute girl with hair that was short in the back and long in the front. She had a gorgeous voice.

I leaned over and asked Thomas how he knew these people. "From school," he whispered in my ear.

"Hey," Anna hissed in my other ear. "Cut it out."

"What?" I said.

"Stop flirting with my brother," Anna said, her eyes blazing in the candlelight.

I couldn't deny it. I *was* flirting with him. Couldn't I have a little fun?

The Smudges played their last song. After packing up their instruments, they dragged over another table and some chairs to join us.

"Great set, Smudges," Thomas said, giving them all high fives.

The girl lead singer sat down on the other side of Thomas, with the rest of the band across from Anna and me.

"Anna and Maddie," Thomas said, "this is Tony and Jeff. And Sam." He turned to the girl.

Thomas and his friends ordered espressos. I ordered another latte and Anna got a Pepsi. Tony and Jeff were cute, almost as cute as Thomas. But not quite. They asked Anna and me how our trip was so far and what we wanted to do.

"Vintage store shopping!" I exclaimed. Tony, Jeff and Thomas guffawed. Then I felt like an idiot for being overly enthusiastic. *Play it cool, Maddie*, I said in my head.

"You going to Screaming Mimi's?" Sam asked, smiling. "That's my favorite store. It's where I got these." She stuck her foot up in the air, revealing the red cowboy boots I'd been admiring.

"Too bad you leave on tour tomorrow," Thomas said to Sam. "You could have taken Maddie shopping."

"Next time she's in New York," Sam said, winking.

Sam asked me what other shops I wanted to visit. Soon I was telling her all about my list of one hundred and thirty-four things I wanted to do. She nodded and asked me smart questions as I went along.

It was official. I wanted to be just like Sam.

As she and I talked, I glanced down and saw that she and Thomas were holding hands.

I felt my heart drop to the top of my stomach, which was sloshing with the three expensive lattes I'd already drunk that night.

Right. Of course the gorgeous, smart, cool Sam was his girlfriend. Silly me.

I felt sweat beads gather on the tip of my nose. That always happened to me when I got embarrassed.

"Are you hot?" Anna said.

"I think I'm just tired," I said.

Anna checked her watch. "Well, we've been awake since four AM local time. Maybe we should go."

We said our goodbyes. Thomas and Sam had a big slurpy kiss right in front of us. Since The Smudges were going on tour the next day, it was the last time Thomas and Sam would be seeing each other for a month. My heart continued to sink.

I didn't say much on the short walk home. The tiredness and the sloshy stomach were hitting me. Apparently the caffeine wasn't.

Back in the apartment, Thomas tucked himself around the corner, half inside a closet.

"I'm comfortable, I swear," he said, his voice muffled. Anna and I laughed, snuggled up on the futon.

"I'm such an idiot," I whispered, a few minutes later, after I heard light snores coming from around the corner. I knew that Anna would know what I was talking about.

"I should have mentioned that Thomas has a girlfriend," Anna whispered back.

A few more moments went by. I decided I'd have to get over it, or I would mope the entire time we were in New York. That would not be cool.

"Tomorrow's my birthday," I said. "Number one on the list for tomorrow: find amazing outfit for the art opening."

"Yay," Anna said, pulling the covers up to her chin. "It'll be a great day.

Sweet dreams." She closed her eyes and was softly snoring in moments.

The city lights in the window shimmered like candles on a birthday cake.

Chapter Five

My eyes popped open at 5:00 AM the next morning. I ran to the window. It was still dark outside. A hint of light poked through a small clump of clouds in the distance.

"I'm fifteen!" I burst out. "And look where I am!" I danced across what space there was on the floor before I stubbed my toe on the corner of a table.

"Ouch!"

Below the floorboards, I heard a muffled yet still loud "shaddup!"

Neither Anna nor Thomas stirred.

My phone vibrated on top of the milk-carton end table. I glanced at the screen. **Happy birthday to my baby girl!**, my mom had written. There were a few other texts that she must have written the night before. I tossed the phone in my bag.

With more rustling than was required, I took my notebook out of my bag. I sat on the corner of the futon and started formulating my list of 19.14 things to do that day. Next to the big *Canvas* art show in three days, this was the most important day of the trip. My fifteenth birthday in New York City was going to be perfect.

I turned to a new page in my notebook and started scribbling down all the vintage stores I wanted to visit.

Anna flopped over to face me. "You have a very loud pencil," she said. Then she hugged me. "Happy birthday!"

"Thank you!" I said, hugging her back. I felt full of sparkles.

Around the corner, I could see Thomas's toes twiddling. A moment later he emerged, hair adorably tousled.

I swallowed. *Forget it, Maddie*, I said in my head.

"Hey, birthday girl!" he said, his voice husky. "What's on your list of 19.14 things to do today?"

Oh, man. Why did he have to be so cute?

I held up my notebook. "Clothes stores, Little Italy, Strand bookstore…"

I trailed off. Thomas had turned around and wandered into the kitchen area. He was rummaging around in the cupboards.

"Sorry, Maddie," he said. "I need my coffee. Major zombie right now."

It took forever to leave the apartment. After cereal and showers, we finally hit the sidewalk.

"It's nine AM," I said, checking my phone. "I hope we have time for everything."

"Maddie, you were the one who had to try on three different outfits and model them for us before we could go out," Anna said.

Thomas gave a soft snort. He looked nervous whenever Anna and I argued.

"I had to look right!" I said.

"You look great," Anna said. "But I still think you're going to regret wearing those shoes."

"Who are you, my mother?" I said. "I love these shoes."

I looked down at my white penny loafers. I had gotten them a week before. Okay, so they weren't broken in yet, but penny loafers were the ideal walking shoes. Plus, they went perfectly with my plaid skirt and button-up blouse with the Peter Pan collar.

My mom had insisted on buying me a pair of sneakers to walk around in. "You see all the New York career gals doing that," she'd said. "They wear their sneakers to work and then put on their high heels at the office!" But there was no way I wanted to look like a fashion "don't."

"Come on, girls!" Thomas said, gesturing for us to go. "Cut the chatter and let's get at 'er. A gal doesn't get to celebrate her birthday in the big city every day."

Anna took my hand and swung it.

"Where to first, b-day gal?" she said.

"Screaming Mimi's is just around the corner," I said.

"Let's go find you that art show dress," Thomas said. "I know nothing about clothes, but I'm here to offer moral support."

He has a girlfriend, I repeated in my head, trying to look cool. *He has a girlfriend.*

"Great," I said. I was full of birthday glee.

Four stores later, though, I was still no closer to finding my perfect art-show outfit. I was nervous. Anna was combing through the racks with me. Even though I hadn't found anything at that point, at least I was having fun.

I came out of the dressing room in Shareen's, a funky shop with vintage designer clothes. I had just tried on a long 1970s dress with bell sleeves and a big flower pattern.

I twirled around, waiting for Anna's and Thomas's opinions.

"Nice," Thomas said. That's what he said to *everything* I tried on. Sweet, but not much help.

"I'm sorry," Anna said. "But it looks like a housecoat."

"That's okay," I said, looking at the price tag. "It's one hundred dollars, anyway." The prices were way steeper than I expected. I thought I'd spend maybe $100 maximum on my art-show outfit, including shoes and accessories. Obviously, it was going to cost more than that.

I tried on a Christian Dior suit. Price tag: $175.

"Nice," Thomas said, glancing up from his phone. He was playing Angry Birds. I could hear the music drifting out of the tiny speakers.

"Are you going to a meeting of the board of directors?" Anna said. "Too corporate for an art opening."

"Yeah, you're right," I said.

"Can't you wear that black dress from home?" Anna said. "That looked really artsy!" She raised her eyebrows and nodded, like she was hoping to make me agree.

"No, I can't!" I said.

"It's just that nothing here is working," Anna said.

"The biggest night of my life is in three days," I said, too loudly. A couple of women flicking through the racks looked over at me. "The true beginning of my career. My introduction to the visual art community of New York. Meeting Louise Bergville, my idol. It's. Really. Really. Important."

Thomas stared intently at his game.

Anna shrugged. "I know how important it is. I think you should wear that black dress."

A sales clerk walked up to us. She was wearing a T-shirt that said: *Oh, the humanity.* "Can I help at all?"

"No, we're okay," I said.

Grumbling, I went back into the dressing room and changed into my own clothes.

"Can we please go eat now?" Anna said when I came back out. "I'm starving."

I pouted.

"I'm sure we'll find your perfect outfit after lunch," she added.

I checked my list and map. My stomach was rumbling too, but I still wanted to try to hit a couple more stores before lunch.

"I'm hungry too," Thomas said, putting his phone in his pocket. "Sorry, Maddie."

I sighed. "There should be a couple of food trucks nearby," I said. "I read about them on the *Food to Go NYC* blog." At least I could check another thing off my list.

After grabbing gourmet hot dogs at the Diggity Dog food truck, we headed over to Fifth Avenue. There was a boutique there with clothes from local indie designers that I wanted to check out.

"Look, Saks Fifth Avenue!" Anna exclaimed. "Let's go in." She headed for the big glass doors.

"No time today," I said, not looking up. I kept walking, fast, right past the doors.

"But maybe you'll find your ideal outfit there," Anna said.

"In a department store?" I scoffed. "No way." I kept walking. My heels were blistering from the loafers, but I wasn't about to tell Anna.

I heard Anna sigh behind me.

"Maddie, can we stop for a minute?" Anna said. She and Thomas were trailing behind me. "We've been non-stop for six hours."

"We still have seven more things to do today," I said, waving my list wildly in the air. "Seven! And it's already three in the afternoon! We haven't even been to an art museum yet."

Finally, I agreed to let Anna and Thomas go into Saks Fifth Avenue and then hang out in a nearby Starbucks while I checked out a row of clothing stores.

"But I promised your mom I wouldn't let you out of my sight," Thomas said, his brows knitted.

"I'll just be around the corner," I said. "We all have our phones, anyway."

"Okay," he said. He looked relieved.

Talk of my mom made me realize she hadn't texted me since the happy birthday message that morning.

I pressed on with the shopping, heels bloody, hobbling around the corner to the next shop. I wished Thomas and Anna were more enthusiastic.

Two hours later, empty-handed, I went back to the Starbucks where Anna and Thomas were waiting. Anna had her head down on the table and Thomas was playing on his phone again. Empty paper cups surrounded them.

I plopped down in a chair next to them. "How can I be in the fashion capital of the world, and I still can't find the right dress?"

"How can it be that I've been sitting in a Starbucks for almost two hours and have drunk five Awake teas, and I still feel tired?" Anna said. "But look," she said, perking up. "*I* found a dress."

She rummaged around in a Saks Fifth Avenue bag.

"For you to wear at my art show?" I asked dumbly.

"Yep," Anna said. She held up a blue silk dress with pleats down the front, and a pattern of tiny white birds on the skirt.

"Oh wow," I said, crestfallen. "It's gorgeous." I couldn't believe Anna had found her dress so easily, and I had nothing.

51

"We'll find something tomorrow," Thomas said soothingly. "Let's go back to my place to change before your big birthday dinner, young lady."

I brightened at that. The day before, Thomas had looked at my list of restaurants. He decided that Myra's, a 1950s-style diner, would be *the* place to go for my birthday dinner.

"Do we still have to dress up?" Anna asked, her voice weak.

Anna seemed grumpy, for some reason. I couldn't believe she could be grumpy when it was my birthday.

"Of course," I said. "I'm going to wear my poodle skirt."

"Anna," Thomas said, "it's Maddie Day today. I, for one, am stoked to slick my hair back and put on my best white T-shirt and jeans."

My stomach flipped. Why was Thomas so nice? It only made things worse.

"I'm stoked too," Anna said, standing up and stretching. "Let's go."

We caught the subway back to Greenwich Village. Even though I was bummed that I hadn't found a dress for the *Canvas* art show, I reassured myself that I still had two more days. The 1950s diner would be fun, like a New York City birthday in a movie. I imagined Anna, Thomas and me all dressed up, laughing in a booth over burgers and milkshakes.

I smiled. There was so much to do, so much to see, it made me perk up again.

It's the Big Apple effect, I thought.

About twenty minutes later, we arrived back at Thomas's apartment. As soon as we got in the door, I kicked off my shoes. My feet were throbbing.

Two steps in the door, we heard rustling in the kitchen.

Anna gasped. "What's that?"

Before any of us could turn on a light, someone jumped out of the kitchen, right in front of us in the darkness.

In the dim light, I saw feet encased in well-worn Reebok sneakers.

"Happy birthday, Maddie!" a too-familiar voice exclaimed.

We all screamed, but I screamed the loudest.

Standing in Thomas's entry, wearing a tie-dyed pantsuit, was my mother.

Chapter Six

"Happy birthday, Maddie!" my mom said again. She flung her arms around me and rocked me from side to side so hard that I bumped my head on the wall.

"I can't believe my baby is fifteen," she said, still rocking. Out of the corner of my eye, I saw Thomas and Anna exchange horrified glances.

When I could, I pulled away. I closed my eyes, willing her to disappear.

After a moment, I snapped my eyes open. No, this wasn't some horrible nightmare. My mother was standing in front of me. In New York City, where I thought I was finally thousands of miles away from her.

"The building superintendent let me in," my mom said. "I explained that I was here to surprise my daughter for her birthday. What a nice man."

Thomas raised his eyebrows and looked at me helplessly.

"I'm sorry," my mom said to Thomas in a sing-song voice. She extended her hand, which he shook. "I should have introduced myself. I'm Lynn Turner, Maddie's mom." To me she mouthed: *cute.*

This was not happening.

I couldn't move. I was too stunned.

"Wow," I said weakly. "I can't believe you're here." My guts churned like I'd eaten a jar of hot banana peppers.

My mom giggled, jumping up and down. "This was my big birthday surprise for you! It was so hard not to tell you. I've been setting aside money for months." She paused, breathless. "Can you believe I'm really here?"

"No, I can't," I said, more weakly.

My legs felt like they weren't working. The room was going blurry all around me, with my mom's clownish, smiling face in the center of it all. Maybe I was about to faint from the worst shock of my life. I had to get out of there.

"I have to go to the bathroom," I said, bolting for the door.

I made my way down the hallway toward the bathroom.

I heard Thomas say, "Uh, would you like some tea, Mrs. Turner?"

I couldn't believe it. My mother had swooped in to ruin the week that I'd saved for, for an entire year. And now Thomas was offering her tea?

I locked myself in the shared bathroom a few doors down the hall. Maybe I'd stay there for a while.

I coughed, and it was like an invitation for the tears to flow. I pounded the grimy brown tiles on the wall.

Ouch. Those tiles were hard.

I heard footsteps. Oh no. I was sure it was *her*.

"Maddie?" a muffled voice said.

"I'm okay," I called through the door.

"It's Anna," the voice called back. "Can I come in?"

Anna. Thank god.

She squished into the tiny toilet room with me. I sat on the closed toilet lid, and she half squatted by the door. It didn't look very comfortable.

"What is she doing here?" Anna said.

Those weren't her only words. What she actually said was a string of every swear word I've ever heard in my life.

"I know," I said. "What the heck?"

Those weren't my exact words either.

I put my hands over my face. "She's here to ruin my life," I croaked through my fingers. "This was supposed to be *my* week in New York. *My* week. Doesn't she know that?"

"Keep it down," Anna said. "We don't want to disturb the creepy dude next door."

I moaned a little less loudly.

"Is that why she kept asking about my brother's address?" Anna said. "So that she could show up here?"

I hadn't thought of that. Of course.

I nodded my head. "What do I do?" I said. Fresh tears were flowing at this point.

"Well," Anna said. "The way I see it, you have three choices."

Sometimes I really appreciated Anna's matter-of-factness. This was one of those times.

"One," she held up her thumb. "Tell her she's not welcome here and to get lost."

"I can't do that," I said. "No matter how much I want to. Would you be able to tell your mom to get lost?"

"My mom would never show up uninvited like this," Anna said.

True that.

"What are my other choices?" I said.

"Two," Anna said. "Ignore her. Silent treatment."

"My mother is impossible to ignore," I said. "You know that."

Anna nodded soberly. "So you can't just tell her how you feel?"

"No," I said. "She won't get it."

"Maybe, in her weird, messed-up way, your mom thought this would be a nice surprise," Anna said.

"I can't believe you would say that!" I glared at the floor.

Anna shrugged. "Just saying."

"She's jealous," I said. "That's what it is. She couldn't handle me going on a summer adventure without her."

"Okay then," Anna said. "Three. You find ways to secretly sabotage her." She had a tiny glint in her blue eyes when she said it.

That made me perk up a little. "That might work," I said.

There was a knock at the toilet door. My mom had finally come looking for me.

"I've been waiting to use the bathroom," a voice boomed from the other side of the door.

"It's the creepy dude!" Anna whispered.

"Do we have to leave now?" I whined.

Anna and I sat hunched in the tiny toilet room, silent. The man kept knocking. I guessed he wasn't willing to go to the other bathroom one floor up.

We slipped out of the toilet room, not looking at the man as we sidled back down the hallway. My stomach was still churning.

Outside the apartment door, I took a deep breath. I asked Anna if my eyes were puffy. Apparently they weren't. It was time to face the music. And that music was my crazy tie-dye-wearing mother singing "New York, New York" to Thomas.

Thomas was leaning against the math poster. His mouth was hanging open. He looked like he'd been stunned by my mother's laser beam of flakiness and high energy.

"Maddie!" my mom said, spinning around. She hugged me again, and then

Anna. "I read my cards on the plane, and I got the Ten of Cups and the Sun. This is going to be the best time ever!"

She hadn't even noticed I'd just locked myself in the bathroom for fifteen minutes. Even though she went on and on about having great awareness, she sure was out of it sometimes.

My mom held up a fan of twenty-dollar bills. "I did a reading for the guy next to me on the plane, and then the woman in front of me was interested, and before I knew it, all of Section E wanted their cards read!"

I couldn't think of a single thing to say. She'd only been there for twenty minutes, and already she'd hijacked the entire trip.

"Dinner's on me!" my mom continued. "We're going to Zelda's Gluten-Free Palace!" Gluten-free was her latest thing. She said it like we were going to Disneyland.

"I think the birthday girl should decide where we go," Anna said, poking me in the back.

"We're going to Myra's," I said. "It's a fifties diner. Burgers and fries, that sort of thing. There's nothing there you can eat." Maybe that would make her stay home. Or go home, all the way back to Vancouver.

"Oh, you know me," my mom said, after a pause. "I'm used to working around the wheat. I'll get the cook to make me something special."

There would be no getting rid of her. Not that easily, anyway.

Chapter Seven

"Don't you have quinoa buns? Or brown rice?"

At Myra's, my mom had already drawn out the ordering for more than ten minutes. They weren't meeting her no-wheat needs. Finally, she ordered a green salad.

"Well," she huffed. "Gluten-free is a common thing these days. You'd think they'd try to accommodate their customers better."

Anna kicked me under the table. She kicked me or grabbed my knee every time my mom said something ridiculous. That meant she was doing it a *lot*.

Ever polite, Thomas didn't even smile. I couldn't help but love Thomas all the more. As soon as my mom showed up, he could have taken off with his friends, but here he was, still hanging out with us. I wasn't sure why he was sticking with us, but I was glad that he was.

Getting out of the apartment had been an ordeal. Anna, Thomas and I had donned our 1950s-themed outfits in honor of the old-style diner. My mom, however, had wanted to wear her tie-dyed wonder. Finally, we convinced her to change into jeans and her least offensive T-shirt, which read: *Keep Calm and Read the Tarot*.

Thomas looked way too hot in his white T-shirt and dark jeans, his hair slicked back. My mom had already whistled and said "hubba-hubba" about his outfit. I couldn't believe she had *hubba-hubba*-ed my friend's brother. Thomas was *my* crush boy. Unavailable, yes, but I had seen him first. She always had to get in there with whatever or whoever I liked.

As we sat in the booth, my mom kept checking her watch. She'd been restless the entire time. All of a sudden, she leapt up.

"Okay, Maddie," she said, breathless, her hands behind her back. "Pick a hand." Her eyes were wide. She looked like she was about to implode with excitement.

"Pick a hand?" I said. This was like when I was little, and sometimes she'd surprise me with a bag of gummy bears. Except this time I had the feeling she wasn't holding any candy.

My mom nodded, looking frantic.

"Um, left?" I said.

Just then, the server arrived with our meals. She started setting down the plates of juicy-looking burgers and fries in front of us.

"Yes!" my mom whipped her hand out from behind her back and held up two tickets. "*Phantom of the Opera*, honey. On Broadway. Second row. Tonight. Happy birthday!"

This big gift of hers showed how little she really knew me.

"Mother," I said, "you should know full well that there is no way I will be dragged into an Andrew Lloyd Webber production."

I looked over at Anna to exchange a can-you-believe-it glance, but Anna was staring at the tickets. Her eyes looked dreamy. I was pretty sure there was some drool coming out of her mouth.

"What?" my mom said. "Maddie, you love theater! I thought you'd be over the moon about this." She sat back down in the booth and took a sip of water. Then she pouted.

"I love theater," I said. "Real theater. Not people, parading around on stage and singing horrible, cheesy songs."

"Second row?" Anna said. "Are you serious?"

"Maddie, don't be silly," my mom said. "I would very much like to take my daughter out to a show on her birthday. I've been saving up all the Lady Venus earnings for months."

That was how my mom usually handled these situations. With guilt, and lots of it.

I shook my head. "Not gonna do it."

This whole time, Thomas had been looking from my mom, to Anna, to me, wide-eyed.

"Well, that's sad," my mom said. Tears dripped out of her eyes. "Really sad."

Like I said, lots of guilt. Still, I hated to see my mom cry. My insides were fighting with each other. *Should I go along with it?* I thought. *No, don't encourage her.*

Anna took a quick breath next to me.

"I'll go with you!" she burst out. Thomas gasped.

"I mean, is that okay, Maddie?" Anna asked. Her eyes were shining. It was a pleading look.

"You're abandoning me on my birthday?" I said. "I can't believe this!"

"We can't let these seats go to waste!" Anna said.

My mom looked like she might cry. Then she looked at her watch again. Time was ticking, and Broadway musicals waited for no one.

"You'll be my honorary daughter tonight," my mom said to Anna, putting her arm in Anna's. "I can see Maddie's got some issues to work through." I hated it when she talked like I wasn't there.

Within moments, they were gone, leaving their unfinished plates, calling back "happy birthday" as they left. I couldn't believe how easily my mom had replaced me with Anna. And I couldn't believe how easily Anna had gone along with my mom.

Now it was just Thomas and me in the booth. Under normal circumstances, that could be fun, but this was not a normal circumstance.

"Yikes," Thomas took a sip of his root beer float. "Remind me to never make you mad."

"Huh?" I looked away from the door that my mom and Anna had just walked through.

"Your glare could cut diamonds right now, I swear," he said.

"How would *you* feel if your so-called friend and mother went to see a show together? On your birthday?" I slapped my hand on the table. Now I didn't know who to be more furious with, my mom or Anna.

"They seemed pretty excited to see *Phantom of the Opera*," Thomas said.

"I can't believe you're taking their side!" I said. "I know Anna's your sister, but think about me for a second here!"

"Sorry," Thomas said. He took another nervous sip of his float.

"My mother is here to ruin my life," I said. That was becoming my new motto. I sucked up the last of my banana-split milkshake so hard that the sound echoed off the ceiling. The server asked if I wanted another. I nodded.

And thus began the rant to end all rants. It seriously went on for a half an hour. Possibly longer.

I found myself telling Thomas the whole story of my mother's craziness. The summer adventures. The raw-food retreat where all we ate was zucchini and kale smoothies. The Wild Wonder Woman Weekend where we were supposed to howl into a hole dug out of the ground. The tarot card readings with Lady Venus. Our week at his family's farm last summer.

The whole time, Thomas looked like he didn't know if he should say anything.

"Did you hear that she feng shui-ed your parents' garden shed?"

Thomas laughed. "My parents are pretty polite people. All they said was that your mom was 'an interesting lady.'" He laughed again. "Anna, on the other hand, told me about it in great detail."

"I know you don't know my mom," I said, "but she seems crazy, right?"

Thomas finally took the bait. "I can't believe she just showed up! I totally didn't know what to do when you and Anna ran off."

Oh right. He was forced to spend at least fifteen minutes of quality Lynn Turner one-on-one time when Anna and I were in the bathroom.

"Sorry about that," I said. "I was in shock."

"Completely understandable," Thomas said. "Almost immediately, she grabbed my palm and told me I'd have three kids and a great love life." He shuddered.

Then we both laughed at the same time. When the server brought me my milkshake, it had a lit birthday candle sticking out of it.

Thomas was the sweetest, cutest boy ever.

"I wish Sam were here," he said with a sigh. "She could sing a proper happy birthday to you."

Thomas was the sweetest, cutest boy ever with a girlfriend.

We finished our milkshakes and then headed home. I felt a little better, at least.

I pretended to be asleep when Anna and my mom got home later that night, giggling and singing "the Phantom of the Opera is here, inside my mind" in ultra-dramatic voices.

Soon enough, my mom rustled into her sleeping bag on the floor, squished up right next to the futon. The apartment fell silent. All was quiet, except for a few sirens and car horns out on the street. That, and my mom's rumbling, garbage-truck-like snores. I pulled the pillow around my ears.

I couldn't sleep anyway. The overwhelming sense of fury and betrayal kept me awake. This was supposed to be the best week of my life, but it was fast becoming one of the worst.

After a while a word popped into my head. *Canvas*. I couldn't forget about the main reason I was there. My big night was only two sleeps away, and I still hadn't found an outfit. With my mom there, I wasn't sure if I ever would.

Chapter Eight

The next morning, I woke up to my mom kneeling next to me, breathing in my face.

"Madison," she said into my ear.

I opened one eye.

"It hurt my feelings that you didn't come to the show with me last night," my mom said.

"I hurt *your* feelings?" I croaked.

My mom sniffed and raised her chin. "I saved up all year for those tickets."

"I saved up all year for this trip," I said, at the exact time that Thomas emerged from the closet, looking adorable and scruffy.

My mom didn't hear me. She was already dragging Thomas over to the table, going on about reading his tarot cards.

I rolled over. Anna wasn't in bed. I figured she must have already been in the shower. I needed to talk to her. Taking a mug of coffee, I waited outside the bathroom.

"Traitor," I said when she came out.

She didn't look at me.

"I can't believe you did that!" If this had been in a movie, I would have splashed the coffee in her face and stormed off. Instead, I just kicked the wall lightly.

"I had fun last night. I've always wanted to see that show," she said.

She said it all in her classic, matter-of-fact way. This only made me angrier.

"It was my birthday!" I half shouted. "You left in the middle of my birthday dinner."

"I had spent all day with you, doing everything you wanted to do," Anna said.

I turned and stomped down the hall. There was nowhere to be alone in Thomas's apartment. I plopped on my stomach on the futon.

I checked my phone. I had a new email.

To: Madison Turner
<artsypunkygirl@grrrlmail.com>
From: Canvas Magazine
<editor@canvasmagazine.com>
  Dear Maddie:
  We look forward to meeting you at the Canvas Youth Portrait Contest art show opening tomorrow evening! A driver will pick you up at the address

**you provided at 6:30 pm to escort you to
the Bolt Gallery.**

Best wishes,

Carl Robertson

Editor, Canvas Magazine

A driver! I couldn't believe it. I felt like a famous artist. I read the email again.

"Anna!" I burst out into the hallway. Then I remembered that she and I had just had a mini-fight. I decided not to care.

"Serious?" Anna exclaimed, when I told her. "Just like in the movies!"

We happy-danced in the hallway.

"Maddie!" my mom called. She was all smiles. "Thomas got the Three of Cups, and you know what that means."

I didn't know and didn't reply.

"He's going to take me shopping," she said.

"I am?" he said. His voice came out like a breathy shriek.

"You're a fashionable city man," my mom said.

"I am?" he repeated. He gave his holey T-shirt and old jeans the once-over. He looked at me.

My mother had never once asked me to help her shop for clothes, despite my in-depth knowledge of European fashion designers. Her flirting with Thomas was beyond sickening.

"But what about *my* dress?" Now I was speaking in a shriek. "I'm looking for my ultimate outfit. I need it by tomorrow night!"

"Maybe we'll find something for you too." My mom put her arm around my shoulder.

"Thomas," Anna called from the doorway. "Can you come here a sec? I think the toilet's plugged."

"I don't know anything about toi—" he started to say, but Anna's stare

81

stopped him. "Coming," he said quickly. Anna cut me a quick glance.

"I'll help," I said. The three of us scurried out.

I decided to put aside my anger toward Anna. I still thought she should apologize, but this was solidarity time. We had to be united against one powerful force: Lynn Turner.

A minute later, the three of us were crammed in the tiny toilet room. This was getting to be a thing.

"She has a minute-by-minute itinerary planned out for each day," Anna said. "It includes doing tai chi and eating organic mung bean sprouts."

I shook my head. "We cannot let her hijack this."

"I kind of feel bad," Anna said. "I went to the play with her and all."

I took Anna by the shoulders. "That was a lapse in judgment," I said.

"We can't let her get away with ruining our trip like this."

"You can leave anytime, Thomas," Anna said. "Don't feel you have to be here for this train wreck."

I could see he was tempted. But then he said, "Some train wrecks are interesting to watch."

We all laughed.

"But what are we going to do about the shopping?" Thomas said, aghast. "I don't know anything about ladies' clothes."

Sometimes, the best ideas come to me in a flash of inspiration. "I know exactly what we're going to do," I said.

I proceeded to lay out my plan of brilliance.

"That seems mean," Thomas said.

Eventually, I convinced them. Thomas took notes on his phone. We all high-fived. This was going to be awesome.

Chapter Nine

The rest of that morning was operation "go along with whatever Lynn wants to do." It looked something like this:

9:53 AM: Lynn reads the palm of a complete stranger on the subway.

10:08 AM: Lynn has a psychic vision of angels on the top of the Empire State Building.

10:47 AM: Lynn asks guy selling newspapers which street Saks Fifth Avenue is on.

11:24 AM: Lynn tells a Starbucks barista that her aura is purple and that love is coming to her soon. The barista just broke up with her boyfriend that morning.

In our past summer adventures my mom had always embarrassed mc in front of hippies. Now she was embarrassing me in front of all of New York City.

Anna, Thomas and I shot each other glances all morning long. After lunch at a raw-food café, it was time for the main part of the plan of brilliance. My arugula, goji berry and nutritional yeast salad still sat like a clump of earthy gloop in my stomach.

We passed store after funky clothes store. It pained me that we weren't able to go into them, considering how desperate I was for my perfect art-show outfit. But I had to stick to the plan. I giggled with diabolical pleasure just thinking about it.

On the Upper West Side we passed a used clothing store called Lulu's. I looked in and saw lots of polyester and crazy prints. I elbowed Thomas.

He didn't miss a beat. "Lynn," he said, turning to my mom and holding out his hand, which she gleefully accepted. "The time to shop is now."

"Really?" she said, peering in the window. "Yay!"

"Remember what I told you," I muttered to Thomas out of the side of my mouth.

Thomas nodded and squared his shoulders. "Let's do this," he said.

Twenty minutes later, a salesgirl had already taken four handpicked Thomas outfits back to my mom's dressing room. He was way better at this than I could ever have expected.

Anna and I sat on a narrow bench next to the mirror by the dressing rooms. Thomas joined us, wiping sweat off his brow.

"You're doing great," I said to Thomas.

After a few minutes my mom came out of the dressing room and twirled around. I had to turn away. There was no way I could hold back my huge smile. She had on a mauve skirt that went almost to the tops of her sneakers, and a blue shirt with silver patches on the shoulders. She looked like a nurse from the Planet Zorgon.

"Looks great," Anna said. She had a wicked poker face. Thomas gave the thumbs-up sign.

My mom checked the price tag. She made a face. "Do you think this looks good on me?" she asked.

"Oh, absolutely," Thomas answered. "Very on-trend." He was getting into it.

She tried on more outfits. In the next one she looked like a librarian from a 1983 Sears catalogue. After that she tried on an orange dress with buttons down the front. Thomas convinced her that the housedress was making a comeback.

"Believe me," he said. "I watch *Project Runway*."

"Well," my mom said, "you're the expert." She handed the Planet Zorgon outfit and the orange housedress to the salesgirl. "I guess I'll take these ones," she said.

I cackled quietly to myself as I headed out to the racks again, looking for more outfits for my mom. Then I felt a tap on my shoulder.

"I don't know how I feel about the plan anymore," Thomas said, his forehead all wrinkled up. Adorably,

I might add. "We're not actually going to let your mom buy those hideous clothes, are we?"

"Yes, we are," I said, flitting past him. "She deserves it after all she's put me through."

As I flicked through a rack of paisley jackets, I spotted a pop of green, above my line of vision. I looked up, and it was like choirs of angels sang from the heavens. Sparkles of light rained down from the skies. Hanging on the wall above the rack was the most gorgeous dress I'd ever seen. It was a luscious deep green, like the skin of a perfectly ripe watermelon. I jumped up and grabbed the dress hanger off the wall.

Please let it be my size, I thought. I checked the tag. *Yes*.

I ran to the dressing room and put it on in about one excited minute. I dashed out to inspect myself in the mirror.

My mom was there, now wearing light blue jean shorts and a coral-colored quilted jacket.

"Wow!" she said. "Maddie!" She stared at me up and down. "If you don't get that dress, I'm going to buy it for you!"

The dress was sleeveless, with a high, loose collar and big pockets. There were oversized black buttons down the front. It would be amazing with black tights, ankle boots and a blue clutch.

Tears pricked my eyes. I felt like I was on one of those shows where the bride finally finds her perfect wedding dress.

Thomas and Anna walked back into the dressing room area. I spun around, speechless.

"Looks nice," Thomas said. "Really nice," he added.

Anna sucked in a breath. "That's it, isn't it?"

I nodded. I had found it at last. My perfect art show-outfit.

I did another spin. I caught a glance of my mom in the mirror, behind me. She looked at me, her eyes shining with motherly love.

I had what I can only describe as a conscience attack.

I turned around and looked my mom over.

"Mom," I said. "I saw a pencil skirt and vintage Chanel blouse that would be perfect for you."

I whisked said items off the rack near the back of the store. On my way to the dressing room, I grabbed a black patent handbag. Gorgeous.

Moments later, my mom came out of the dressing room again. This time, no alien costume or ugly librarian outfit.

Mom looked like a knockout.

Thomas, Anna and I made all the appropriate *oohs* and *ahs*.

She looked at herself in the mirror like she'd never seen herself before.

Then Anna whispered to me, "What the heck? What about your plan of brilliance?"

"I dunno," I said. "Something came over me."

"Sometimes I don't understand you," Anna said, shaking her head. "But you did the right thing."

I had found my perfect outfit, with one day to spare. I sailed through the rest of the day. I didn't even groan when my mom tried to haggle over a pair of socks at the front counter.

I hadn't forgiven her, not even close, but I felt like being generous with the whole world at that moment.

Unfortunately, the feeling would turn out to be temporary.

Chapter Ten

The next day, it was just my mom and me.

"Thomas and I are going to do some brother-and-sister stuff this morning," Anna had announced at breakfast.

"Like what?" I asked.

"Central Park," Anna said. "Typical touristy stuff."

Thomas didn't meet my eyes. Maybe he felt guilty. Anna didn't seem to.

We agreed to meet outside the Guggenheim Museum at two o'clock.

Thomas and Anna left, and Mom was in the shower. I lay on my stomach on the futon. This was the day I'd been anticipating for a whole year, but this wasn't quite what I'd imagined.

Part of me felt abandoned. Part of me, though, could understand why Anna and Thomas wanted some sibling time on their own. They hadn't seen each other in a year. Also, things had been pretty crazy the past few days. I wished I had a brother or sister to hang out with—someone else who'd understand how nuts my mom was.

I took out my notebook with my list of all the things I'd wanted to do in the city. Of the one hundred and thirty-four things, I'd done only twenty-six. There were only two and a half days left. I quickly did some math on my phone. If I wanted to do everything before I left,

I would have to do 43.2 things per day. I hadn't been to Brooklyn yet, or to any museums, or to Strand Bookstore.

I hadn't told my mom about all the things I wanted to do. My trip to New York had been so special to me that I hadn't shared it with her. I didn't think she'd get it.

If I wanted to have any chance of doing 43.2 things that day, though, I decided I had to.

Surprisingly, my mom was into checking out galleries. "I like art," Mom said, "I sure do like that Andy Warhole." She pulled up her leggings under her peasant skirt. Despite the awesome outfit I'd found for her the day before, she insisted on donning her hippie gear again.

"*Warhol*, Mom, Warhol." It was going to be a long day.

We took the subway to the Museum of Modern Art. My mom only tried to give one old lady a reiki treatment during the ride.

Maybe this will turn out okay, I thought. I was actually pleased at the chance to give my mom a glimpse into my love of art. Maybe it would give her a better understanding of my passions.

The Museum of Modern Art was my very own heaven. I gasped at everything, from the high ceilings in the galleries to the Picasso paintings. My mom thought Frida Kahlo's paintings were "weird" and Matisse's were "interesting."

"Don't you love his attention to texture?" I said to my mom, gazing at a Jackson Pollock, with its splotches of paint covering a huge canvas.

"Mom?" I said, glancing around. She had just been with me.

I didn't see her. But then, moments later, I heard her laugh.

My mom doesn't laugh like a regular person. It starts out like a honking guffaw and quickly becomes a series of pig snorts when she really gets going. I heard the pig snorts echoing around the corner, near the Warhol exhibit.

There, in front of the famous painting of the tomato soup can, was my mom. She was standing with another lady who looked just like my mom. The lady had long, scraggly blond hair with a sparkly blue scarf tied in it and silver rings on every finger. She wore a long flowy skirt and a leather vest.

They looked like a new exhibit at the museum: "Fortysomething New Age Hippies of the Pacific Northwest."

I tried to hide behind a post, but my mom spotted me. She ran over, towing her lookalike by the hand.

"This is Raven Moonlove," my mom said, still gripping the lady's hand. "My daughter, Maddie."

"You have beautiful eyes," Raven Moonlove said, touching my cheek. "Oh, she's an old soul," she said to my mom.

My mom smiled hugely. "Raven's learning how to find her animal medicine guide. And she's a *fortune-teller*," she added, eyes wide.

Raven Moonlove laughed. "Future consultant," she said.

I couldn't believe it. They'd been talking a grand total of two minutes, and she already knew all this about her?

Raven spread her arms wide and tipped her head back. "I had to come in and soak up the energy in this space. It's amazing." Then she proceeded to sway and lunge, and do some sort of modern dance routine, right in the middle of the gallery.

My mom was looking on admiringly. Then, what did she do? She joined in. The two of them started twirling around each other, swept away in the moment.

My mom moaned a little as she dipped and twirled, eyes closed. An older couple snapped a photo.

I hid again. This was quite possibly the most surreal moment of my life. Standard torture would have been welcome at that moment.

After they finished their dance, Raven Moonlove and my mom hugged and then laughed. My mom's snort echoed all the way through the fourth floor.

I had to get away. There was no way I could spend the next two hours with them.

"Mom, I think I'll go—" I started to say.

"We're going to go meditate in the Architecture and Design exhibit," my mom interrupted, arm in arm with her new best friend. "See you in the gift shop at one thirty?"

I nodded, stunned. Mom and Raven swished off in their long skirts.

I plopped down on a bench. I'd finally gotten rid of my mom for a while, but it didn't feel as satisfying as I'd thought it would. I had hoped that my mom would finally understand my world better. Instead, she'd ditched me for a fortune-teller. I mean, future consultant.

I wandered through galleries of Van Gogh and Monet paintings. This was what I'd been dreaming of for a year, but now I was bitter instead of happy.

Soon enough, it was time to meet up at the gift shop. Raven Moonlove and my mom were now talking about getting matching foot tattoos.

"With swirls down to our toes, to represent the feminine mystical," Raven Moonlove said. My mom nodded sagely.

We rode the bus to the Guggenheim Museum to meet Anna and Thomas. I couldn't wait for them to get a load of what my mom had picked up.

On the bus, my mom turned to me as Raven Moonlove was reading another passenger's energy. "Isn't she such a neat lady?" she said. "I love having someone that I can connect with."

"Yeah, that's great," I said in a monotone. It was always the same. On every summer adventure before that, except for Anna's farm, my mom had always found someone else to be best friends with, and then left me in the dust.

After twenty aching minutes, we reached the Guggenheim. There were Anna and Thomas, wearing those "I Heart NY" hats and laughing with each other. I'd never been so happy to see two people in my entire life.

Their mouths snapped shut as soon as they saw us. Thomas gave Raven Moonlove the twice-over, his eyebrows creased together.

"Raven and I are going to go to Zelda's Gluten-Free Palace," my mom said. "She's GF too."

"Gluten is poison," Raven said, eyes closed. She talked with her eyes closed a lot. "Absolute poison."

Off they went, with my mom wishing me luck for my big night. Mom would see me back at Thomas's later that night.

Thomas and Anna watched them go.

"What was that?!" Thomas said, still staring.

"Well, you got rid of your mom," Anna said, putting her hand on my shoulder. "You're happy now, right?"

I nodded. I told them about the modern dance routine.

Anna's lips were quivering in the corners. She couldn't hold it in. Next she was bending at the waist, wheezing with laughter. Thomas put his hand over his mouth, but he couldn't hold in the guffaw.

Pretty soon, I stopped feeling sorry for myself. I was too busy doubled over with laughter.

"I can't believe people like that lady actually exist," Thomas said, once he was able to stop laughing.

I felt better after that.

In front of us, the white museum building towered in all its circular majesty.

"Ready to rock the Guggenheim?" Thomas said.

I nodded and then checked my watch. The big *Canvas* art show was only four hours away.

Chapter Eleven

I looked at myself in the mirror again. Dangly asymmetrical earrings, check. Perfect art-show dress, check. Subtle eyes and strong red lips, check. Smooth hair, check.

I emerged from behind the closet door, where I'd been prepping. Anna was already wearing her new dress, with her long red hair piled up on top of her head in a sloppy bun. She looked amazing.

I walked the three steps to the table like I was walking the catwalk. "Do I look ready to meet my destiny?" I said.

"Classy lady!" Thomas whistled. He was so cute and old-fashioned that he used dorky sayings like "classy lady." Anna clapped.

In a weird way, I wished my mom was there. I wanted her to have a proud moment for me. But she was probably healing the chakras of the Central Park ducks with Raven Moonlove.

The clock on Thomas's stove read 6:10. Only twenty minutes until the driver was to arrive.

In an hour, people from the New York art world would be looking at my portrait. I imagined them fawning over me and my work. I bet they'd want to book me for an exhibit at the Metropolitan

Museum of Art. Goose bumps shivered down my arm.

"Anna, are you okay?" Thomas's voice snapped me out of it.

Anna had her hand to her mouth. She shook her head. Sweat had broken out on her forehead. She stood up and ran out the door.

"Uh-oh," said Thomas, watching her go.

When she didn't come back in five minutes, Thomas and I went to check on her.

"That doesn't sound good," Thomas said. Retching sounds echoed down the hall from the bathroom.

Anna had her head over the dirty, gross toilet. She must have been really sick to be okay with that.

"Hey, sis," Thomas said, rubbing her back. He was so sweet, even in a crisis.

"I bet it was that pizza we had in Times Square," Anna croaked, lifting her head up for a second.

"Those will get you every time," Thomas said, still rubbing her back. "Maddie, could you go get her a glass of water?"

I rushed back to the kitchen and poured Anna some water in a chipped coffee mug.

Speed walking back to the bathroom, I started to feel a bit ill myself. I knew Anna couldn't help being sick, but what was I going to do about the big show?

"Does this mean you can't come?" I said, passing the mug of water. I checked the time on my phone. 6:23.

"Not unless you want me to barf all over the art," Anna said. "I'm sorry, Maddie. I was really looking forward to—" She retched again.

I couldn't imagine myself going alone. "Thomas, can you come with me?" I asked, feeling desperate.

Thomas looked at me like I had three heads all of a sudden. "Uh, no," he said. "I need to stay here with Anna."

With great reluctance, I left. The car, with the words *Canvas Magazine* tastefully printed in the back passenger window, was waiting for me when I went downstairs. As I slid onto the buttery leather seat, I wanted to feel giddy and excited. But it was hard without my best friend there.

When I arrived at the Bolt Gallery, the room was already abuzz. Carl Robertson, the editor of *Canvas Magazine*, greeted me at the door. He was exactly as I imagined: short brown hair, stylish glasses and a gray suit.

"It's one of our VIPs!" he said, putting his arm around me and ushering me in. He fussed about me coming alone, and then said that I'd make new friends there. A girl took my coat, and then Carl dropped a glass of sparkling water into my hand with an air kiss before running off to greet someone else. I felt so special.

Even though Anna wasn't there, I had to drink in the moment. The Bolt Gallery was a huge loft space. The prizewinning portraits lined one wall. A DJ was spinning some mellow beats in the corner. A long banner stretched across one wall: *Canvas Magazine presents the "Face of Youth" Art Contest Winners.*

I'd studied Louise Bergville's photo on her website so that I'd be sure to spot her right away. I looked around for the gray bobbed hair and big black glasses. Nothing. Maybe she wasn't there yet.

A server came by with a plate of crackers with various fancy spreads on them. I took one with cream cheese, and proceeded to drop a blob right down the front of my dress. Crap. At that very moment, another girl about my age and an older woman rushed up to me.

"Are you Maddie?" the girl said, as I tried to subtly wipe the blob off my front.

"I'm Jessie Sayers," she said, flipping her hair. "Like, the first prize winner? Can we do a selfie?"

Before I knew it, Jessie had wrapped her arm around my shoulder and pointed her phone in our faces. *Flash.* Great. My cream cheese blob was probably going to end up on her Facebook page. Jessie ran off, likely to find her next victim.

Seeing my portrait gave me electric shivers down my back. I hadn't seen it since I'd left it, propped up against Anna's bedroom door. I wished Anna could be there to see the portrait of her cow, Frida Cowlo. I marveled at the detail I'd put in, from her eyebrows to the flowers on her head.

The chatter in the room began to die down. Carl Robertson was at the microphone, greeting everyone and introducing the winners. When he said my name, I put my hand up and everyone turned to look at me and clapped.

I could feel the red rise from underneath my dress collar all the way up to my hairline. I hoped no one noticed.

So this is what it feels like to be a celebrity, I thought.

"We're sorry that one of our guests of honor, Louise Bergville, couldn't make it tonight." Then Carl started chatting on about something else.

No Louise Bergville. My heart thunked into my stomach. I hadn't even thought of the possibility of her not being there.

Carl finished his speech and the crowd started buzzing again. I snuck around the corner behind the wall of portraits, trying to gather myself together. It was the second time that day that I'd hidden in an art gallery.

Two women about my mom's age, maybe older, were looking at the winning portraits. One was very thin with bright red hair, wearing an all-black jumpsuit. The other one was curvier, with long brown hair and a polka-dot dress. I recognized them as Trish and Toni from *The Stick and the Stone*, a visual art–review blog that I loved.

My heart fluttered. They weren't Louise Bergville, but these ladies were pretty darn cool. When they paused on my painting, I sucked in a breath.

Toni's mouth twisted. She squinted.

"Oh, these hopeful, naïve young artists," she said. "Drawing pictures of…farm animals?"

"Uninspired," Trish said with a sigh.

Toni made a flicking motion with her hand. "Derivative."

I didn't know what that meant, but my heart thunked even lower. Trish and Toni moved on to the next portrait. I didn't hear what they said about it, but Toni made the same flicking motion.

Everything that had happened to me that day seemed to crash together at once. My crazy mom. No Anna. No Louise Bergville. My art was ugly. Tears sprang to my eyes.

"Do you always hide behind walls at art openings?"

I whipped my head around. A boy was standing next to me. I hadn't even noticed him.

I looked down. I didn't want this guy, whoever he was, to see my tears. I quickly wiped them.

"Timber," he said, extending his hand. I only glanced at him, but he looked about my age.

"Maddie," I said, shaking his hand and looking down again. I kind of wanted him to go away.

"Um," he said. "Are you okay?"

What did he care? "Yeah," I said. "I just want to be back here for a minute."

My phone buzzed in my pocket. **Maddie! Call me!** A text from my mom. She'd probably had a psychic break-through about her aura and had to tell me. I put my phone back in my pocket.

Timber was still standing there. I glanced up. He was looking around the room. He *tsked*. "*The Stick and the Stone* people are here. My mom can't stand them. She says they wouldn't know a good work of art if it bit them on the bum."

I looked up. "They called my portrait 'derivative' and 'uninspired.'" I could barely get the words out.

"Yours is the cow, right?" he said.

I nodded, feeling unsure about it by that point. Did he hate it too?

My phone buzzed again. I pulled it out. My mom was phoning me. I put it back in my pocket, still buzzing.

"Do you need to answer that?" Timber said. I shook my head.

"So, are you one of the contest winners too?" I said. He was cute. More than cute. More like out-of-my-league hot. He was a little taller than me, with longish sandy blond hair and blue eyes.

"No," he said. "My mom was supposed to be here, but then she had to go open a gallery in Tokyo. I came in her place." He said it like it was normal to jet off to Japan at a moment's notice.

My mouth fell open as my brain quickly assembled all the pieces.

"Y-y-y-y—" I couldn't say it. I was totally dumbstruck. "Your mom is Louise Bergville."

A tall woman wearing a headset bustled up to us. "Madison Turner?" she said. "Urgent phone call for you. This way."

I turned to Timber. "Don't go anywhere," I said.

The woman rushed me off to a small back room.

"Maddie!" my mom screamed over the phone. "I'm lost! Why weren't you picking up your phone?"

"I'm at my big show, Mom," I said. "How did you get this number?" But she couldn't hear me. She was sobbing too loudly.

"Raven ditched me to follow her animal spirit," she cried. "That was somewhere back in Chinatown. Now I don't even know where I am."

I tried to remain calm. "Go look at the nearest street signs. Then Google Map it and find your way back to Thomas's place."

"I can't," she wailed. "I don't know how to do that. I need your help."

Serves her right, I thought, *for ruining my trip.* I thought of leaving her there.

"Please." She paused. "I think someone's following me." She screamed.

Maybe she was faking it, but the guilt had clutched my chest. I didn't want to go, but I knew I had to.

Chapter Twelve

As it turned out, my mom wasn't lost at all. When we finally found her, huddled in a coffee shop, she was only a few blocks from Thomas's apartment.

I'd recruited Thomas to come help me find her. Anna had gone to bed, still sick.

"Maddie," my mom said, mascara streaking down her cheeks. "I was so scared."

I didn't want to hear it. Any of it.

I turned around and stalked out of the coffee shop, with Thomas and then my mom close behind.

"Maddie," my mom was still whining behind me. "Raven *abandoned* me."

"Do you think I *care*?" I said, turning on her. "You have ruined my entire night. I'd just met Louise Bergville's son when you pulled me away!"

After my mom had called, I'd rushed out of the party. I didn't have any way to contact Timber. Now I felt even worse. And that much more furious.

My mom sniffed. "I thought you'd be worried about me."

I glanced at Thomas. He looked uncomfortable, like he had a big itch that he couldn't scratch.

"Uh," he said, "I'll meet you back at home." I didn't blame him.

"Mom, you didn't just ruin my night," I said. "You've ruined my entire *trip*."

We were walking and fighting. My mom kept trying to stop me, but I kept walking.

"Oh, hon," she said. "I thought you'd love having your old mom show up. That's all." She started crying again.

There she went, laying on the guilt again.

"This was *my* trip," I said, poking my finger into my chest. "My first time getting to do what I want to do. And you still managed to make it all about you!"

"Well, that wasn't my intention, Maddie," my mom said. "I hope you can understand that."

"I hope you can understand *me*," I said.

We had reached the front steps of Thomas's building. My mom raised her arms over her head in a yoga sun salutation.

"I need to be one with myself for a few minutes," she said, closing her eyes.

I was happy to leave her outside. As the door banged behind me, I could hear her chanting.

Anna was sitting up on the futon when I walked in, wrapped in a blanket. Thomas was sitting on the futon next to her.

"How are you feeling?" I said.

"Better," she said. "How was the show?"

I told her. Everything. Thomas had already filled her in on the hunt for my lost mother.

"Jeez," Anna said. "I can't believe she pulled you away from your big show like that. And you got to meet what's-her-name's son?"

I nodded. I didn't want to tell Anna how cute he was in front of Thomas.

"But I'll probably never speak to him again." I flopped on the futon next to Anna. I felt the rage building again. I went on another full-on, my-mom-has-ruined-my-life rant.

"She hasn't let me do anything I wanted to do," I said, leaning on my elbow on the futon.

Thomas got up and ran to the window. "She's still down there," he said. "She's waving her arms in the air and chanting. A small crowd is gathering."

"STOP!" Anna said. She pounded her fist on the futon. I sat up.

"Stop," Anna said again. "Maddie, I have had *enough*."

"Huh?" I said. What was Anna talking about?

"Your mom hasn't let *you* do anything *you* wanted to do?" Anna laughed. It was a hard, mocking laugh. "Maddie, today was glorious. *Glorious*. Other than puking, of course. I finally got to have fun. We went to the zoo. We did touristy things. All the other days,

I've been dragged around doing things from your list of the zillion things you wanted do." Her eyes were wild. Anna didn't usually lose her cool.

"I thought you wanted to do those things," I said.

"I was trying to be nice! It was your birthday, and then it was your big art show. I was happy for you, really I was! But I saved up for this trip too. It's my trip as much as it is yours," she said.

"You went to see *The Phantom of the Opera*," I said, pointing an accusing finger at her.

"Who cares about *The Phantom of the Opera*," she said. "That was three out of seventy-two hours of boredom and shopping torture."

Thomas was still looking intently out the window, avoiding the fight, of course.

"You've spent so much time ranting to me," Anna went on, "about how your mom has dragged you on summer adventures where she doesn't care what you want to do and only does what she wants to do."

"Yeah, like now," I said.

"I hate to say it, but…" Anna said.

"But what?" I said. Anna didn't respond. She looked at me, one eyebrow raised.

Boom. I got it.

I wanted to run outside. I wanted to escape the room, the building, this ruined trip. But I couldn't. My mom was out there.

So I went to my usual hiding place. The bathroom.

I stayed there for I don't know how long. I hadn't brought my phone in with me. I didn't know what time it was. I hummed. I looked up at the cracks in the ceiling. No one came to check on me. No one came at all.

At first, I wasn't ready to think about what Anna said. But after a while, her words started to ring around in my head.

I hated to admit it, but thinking back over the past few days, I could see what Anna was saying. I had dragged her all around the city for three whole days.

In my efforts to get away from my mom that summer, to do something totally different, I'd become exactly like my mom.

The rage that I'd felt toward my mom, I now felt toward myself.

I had to sit with that a while.

When I was ready, I leapt off the closed toilet lid. My butt was numb from sitting there so long.

With a flourish, I opened the door to Thomas's apartment. It was dark. I had hoped to do a big, dramatic, soul-baring speech, but everyone was asleep.

My mom was on the floor. Surprisingly, she wasn't snoring.

"Maddie," Anna said in a sleepy voice. "You were gone for like two hours."

No wonder my butt hurt so much.

I knelt down next to Anna.

"Anna," I whispered. She raised her head. "I'm sorry. I'm an idiot. I did make this trip all about me."

Hot tears were brimming out of my eyes, but Anna wouldn't be able to see them in the dark.

"You're not an idiot," she said after a moment. "And stop crying." She patted my hair. On the floor, my mom rustled around.

"I'm really, really sorry," I tried to sob as quietly as possible. I didn't want my mom to hear.

"I accept your apology," Anna said. "It's okay. I'm sorry that I overreacted tonight."

"You didn't," I said. "I deserved it."

I crawled over Anna to my side of the futon. I fell asleep, more exhausted than I'd been in years.

We slept in the next morning. We all needed it.

I was the first one to wake up. It was a bright, blue-sky day.

I blinked and looked around. There was a blank spot on the floor where my mom had been in her sleeping bag. I sat up.

On the table there was a note written on a coffee filter.

Took an earlier flight home. Have a date with the Big Apple.

Love, Mom

Tucked inside the coffee filter was one hundred dollars. I gasped. Then I woke up Anna and Thomas, of course.

Thomas said it was the classy thing for my mom to do. Anna couldn't believe it.

I felt a little guilty about my mom leaving early, but not really. I kept wondering, though, had she heard me the night before?

We decided to hang out in the apartment for a bit before heading out.

I checked my email on my phone. When I saw my inbox, I felt like my eyes were boing-ing out of my head. There was an email from Timber.

"Timber!" I shrieked to Anna and Thomas. "He sent me an email!"

To: Madison Turner
<artsypunkygirl@grrrlmail.com>
From: Timber Bergville
<fallingtrees@mailbox.com>
    Hi Maddie,
    I was sad that I missed saying goodbye to you last night. Carl from Canvas gave me your email. I said I had to contact you for business reasons, which is partly true. My mom wants to

buy your portrait to hang in her library. It's her favorite one.

I'm in Cape Cod for the weekend, but my mom has an exhibit coming to the Vancouver Art Gallery in October. I hope you can show me your city then. If you want to.

Ciao,

Timber

Wow. *Wow*. That was all I could think for about three straight minutes. Had I just rubbed a magical genie lamp? Were all my wishes coming true?

Had a boy as hot as Timber actually gone to the trouble of getting my email?

Yes, yes he had.

Of course, I read the email out to Thomas and Anna. I then read it again to myself, probably two dozen times.

"He sounds rich," Anna said. "And his mom wants to buy your art!"

I blushed. I felt like I was betraying Thomas, but that was ridiculous. He had a girlfriend he was madly in love with.

"We have to celebrate," Thomas said. "The world's our oyster." He pointed to my notebook on the table.

"So," Thomas continued, his voice a little weak. "We can do 47.2 things today, right?"

I opened the garbage can and thwacked my notebook into it. It closed with a clang. Anna and Thomas looked at me and then looked at each other.

"Forget it," I said. "What do you guys want to do?"

"Quite honestly," Thomas said. "I could go for a Big Mac right now."

Anna mmmmm-ed. "I think some fries are calling my name."

"Two cheeseburgers, please," I said, smiling.

Arm in arm, we skipped out the door and into the light of the Big Apple.

ACKNOWLEDGMENTS

A huge thank-you to my wonderful editor, Melanie Jeffs. This is the third book we've worked on together, and I am forever appreciative of her thoughtful edits. Massive gratitude and smooches to my husband, Joshua, my faithful first reader and sounding board, and to my fabulous writing group, the Inkslingers. Much thanks, as always, to my family.

The Big Apple Effect is Christy Goerzen's second novel featuring Maddie and her crazy mom. In the first novel, *Farmed Out*, the two wreak havoc at Anna's family's farm. Christy lives in Vancouver, British Columbia, with her husband and two children.